This book belongs to

....

....

A catalogue record for this book is available from the British Library
Published by Ladybird Books Ltd.
A Penguin Company
80 Strand, London, WC2R 0RL, England
Penguin Books Australia Ltd, 250 Camberwell Road,
Camberwell, Victoria 3124, Australia
New York, Canada, India, New Zealand, South Africa

001 - 10 9 8 7 6 5 4 3 2 1

© Eric Hill, 2004
This edition published 2011
Eric Hill has asserted his moral rights under the
Copyright, Designs and Patents Act of 1988
All rights reserved
Planned and produced by Ventura Publishing Ltd
80 Strand, London WC2R 0RL

ISBN 978-0-72326-756-0

Printed in China

Spot

and his
Grandma

Eric Hill

Spot's mum and dad were going out for a little while and Grandma was going to stay with Spot till they got back.
"We'll have fun, won't we, Spot?" said Grandma.
"Yes!" agreed Spot happily, as he waved goodbye to Mum and Dad.

"What would you like to do today, Spot?" Grandma asked, as they went back inside.

"I have a new jigsaw," said Spot. "Will you help me to put it together?"

"Of course," said Grandma, "but first you'll have to help me find it."

"I think it might be on the top shelf of the bookcase," said Spot.

Grandma looked on all the shelves of the bookcase. Then she looked in the hall cupboard. "I can't seem to find the jigsaw, Spot," she said. "Where do you think it could be?"

"Grandma, I think the jigsaw must be playing hide-and-seek," said Spot, following Grandma back into the living room.
"I think you're right, Spot," said Grandma. "And I think I know where it might be hiding!"

She crouched down to look under
a chair.
"Found it!" she said.

Grandma needed a cup of tea after all that looking, and Spot had some milk and biscuits. Then, at last, they settled down to put the jigsaw together.

Spot finished it very quickly!
"I think you'll have to give me
some lessons, Spot," said
Grandma. "I'd love to be able to
put a jigsaw together as quickly
as you!"

Spot wanted to play a game next. "Looking for the jigsaw was fun! Please can we play hide-and-seek now? Do you think you'll be able to find me, Grandma?"

"I'll do my best, Spot," she said.
She closed her eyes and counted
to twenty, to give Spot a chance
to find a good hiding place.
"Don't peek!" called Spot.

Grandma looked for Spot in his bedroom. She looked for him in Mum and Dad's bedroom, too. She even looked in the airing cupboard. But Spot wasn't there.

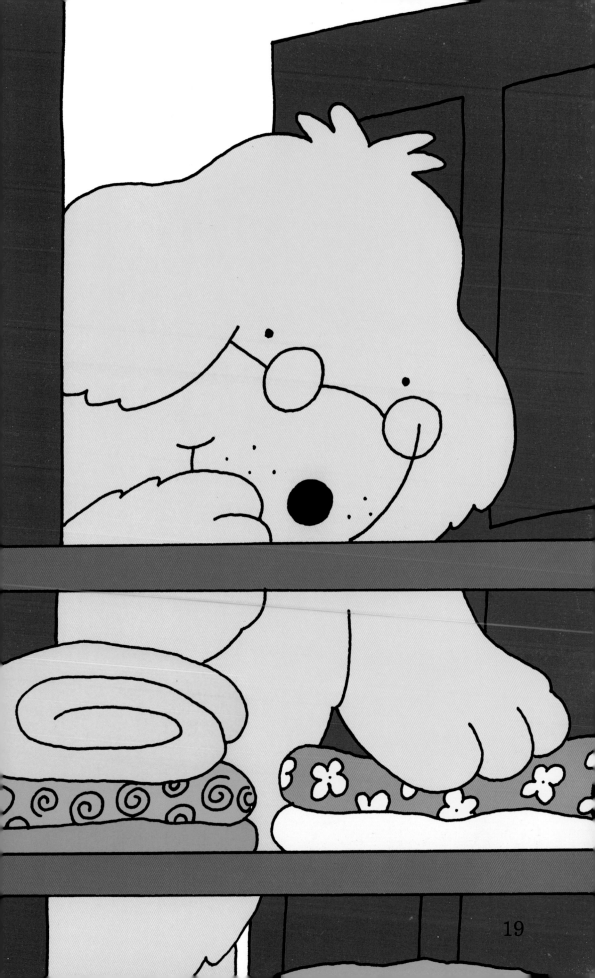

Grandma went downstairs to look for Spot. She looked in the cupboard under the stairs.

Grandma even looked for Spot
outside in the garden.
"Spot is good at hide-and-seek,"
she said to herself. "I can't find
him anywhere!"

Grandma came back inside. "I think I need a little rest before I keep looking," she said to herself, sitting down on the sofa. Then..."What's that scuffling?" she wondered, turning to look. Suddenly, UP popped Spot.

"Here I am, Grandma!" he said.
"You couldn't find me, could you?"
"No, Spot," laughed Grandma.
"I think you've won this game."

Just then the front door opened.
Mum and Dad were home.
"Hello, Mum and Dad!" said Spot,
rushing to greet them.
"Hello, Spot!" they said, giving
him a hug. "Did you have a good
time with Grandma?"

"Grandma and I had a wonderful time," said Spot. "I hope she can stay and play some more games with me. Can you, Grandma?"
"I think I'll have a rest for now," said Grandma.
"Maybe we can play a resting game together," said Spot, snuggling up next to her.
"That's a very good idea," Grandma replied, giving Spot a cuddle. "I think I like that game best of all!"